Published in the United States by Grolier Books, a division of
Grolier Enterprises, Inc.

First American Edition.

ISBN: 0-7172-8823-4

Disney's Pooh

How to Catch a Heffalump

R. SANDERS

GROLIER
BOOKS

It was a beautiful, bird-singing, picnic
kind of day in the Hundred-Acre Wood.

"Where shall we have our picnic,
Christopher Robin?" asked Piglet.

"I'm not sure. We'll stop when we
find a good picnic spot," answered
Christopher Robin.

"Oh, let's stop here!" declared Pooh.

"How do you know this is a good picnic spot?" wondered Christopher Robin.

"My tummy says that it's time to stop for lunch. And our lunch is in the picnic basket. So I think this must be a good spot for a picnic."

"Silly old bear," laughed Christopher Robin.

The friends spread out the red-and-white cloth on the ground. It was a friendly, bird-feeding and honey-eating kind of picnic.

"You know," Christopher Robin said, pointing. "I thought I saw a heffalump right over there."

"A heffalump?" said Piglet. "W-w-where?"

Piglet was not quite sure what a heffalump was. But Piglet thought it sounded like a very large animal.

"It's not there now," said Christopher Robin. "I thought I saw one yesterday. I wish I had caught it. Then I could have shown it to you."

"That would have been nice," Pooh said.

When they had finished
their lunch, Christopher
Robin had to go home.
Christopher Robin
waved. "Good-bye, Pooh.
Good-bye, Piglet."
"Good-bye," called
Pooh and Piglet as they
waved back.

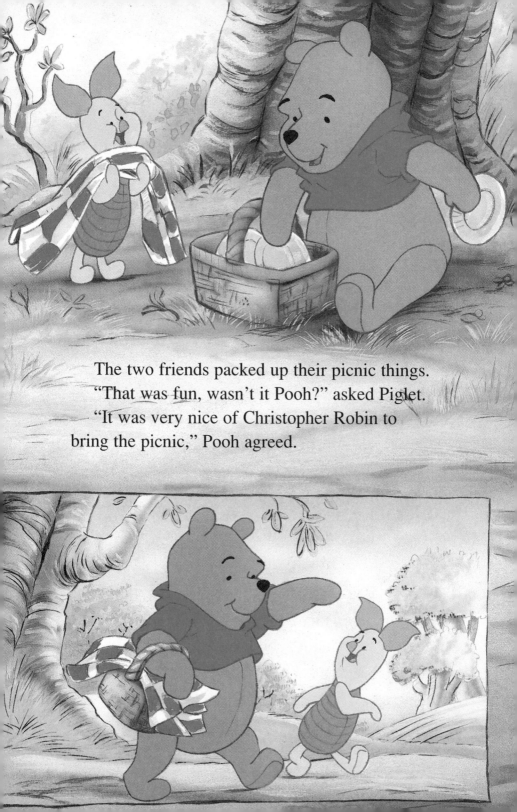

The two friends packed up their picnic things.
"That was fun, wasn't it Pooh?" asked Piglet.
"It was very nice of Christopher Robin to
bring the picnic," Pooh agreed.

"Perhaps we could do something nice to thank him," Pooh said.

"What a good idea, Pooh. What should we do?" wondered Piglet.

Pooh thought for a moment.

"I know. We shall catch a heffalump
for Christopher Robin!" Pooh shouted happily.

"A h-h-heffalump?" Piglet asked nervously.
"Isn't that awfully dangerous, Pooh?"

"Perhaps," Pooh replied.
"Heffalumps are clever
animals, I think. We
need a clever plan."

So the two friends sat down
to think of a clever plan.
"Think, think, think," said Pooh,
tapping his head.
"Could we set some sort of trap?"
wondered Piglet.

That seemed like a very clever plan to Pooh.
But what sort of trap? He stood up and began
to draw in the dirt.

"We could dig a deep hole," Pooh said.
"And the heffalump would fall into the hole."

"Where would we dig the hole?" Piglet asked.

"Exactly where the heffalump would fall
into it," Pooh answered.

He drew a picture of the hole under a tree.

"Won't the heffalump see the hole?" asked Piglet. "They are very clever animals. At least, I think they're clever."

"No," answered Pooh. "The heffalump will be looking up, so he won't see himself fall down."

Piglet smiled.

"Yes," he said, "that is a very good plan. Heffalumps are always looking up."

Piglet did not really know if heffalumps always looked up or not, but he thought they did.

One problem still remained—how would
they lure the heffalump to the hole?

"I know!" said Piglet excitedly. "Heffalumps
are very large, so they must eat a lot of food!"

Piglet drew a heffalump in the dirt to show
Pooh how big it was. Or at least how big he
thought it was.

"Maybe it would come to the hole if there
was food," said Piglet. "But what food do
heffalumps like, Pooh?"

Piglet turned around to find that
Pooh had fallen asleep!
All this heffalump talk had tired
out the bear's little brain!
"Pooh?" said Piglet.

"Yes?" said Pooh sleepily.

"What do you think a heffalump likes to eat?" Piglet asked.

Pooh thought of the only food he ever thought of. "Honey," he replied.

"Yes!" Piglet said excitedly. "That is a good idea. Heffalumps like honey."

At least he thought they did.

"Hooray!" Piglet cried. "We have a clever plan!"

So they decided that Pooh would go home to get a pot of honey.

Meanwhile, Piglet would get a shovel to dig the hole.

When Pooh got home,
he opened his cupboard.
"This pot is far too
heavy to carry," he said.

So Pooh decided to remove some
of the honey. And since he did not
have anywhere to put the
honey, he put it in
his mouth.

The honey pot was still heavy. So, as
he walked along, Pooh ate some more.

Then he ate some more again.

And again. And again.

As Pooh walked to meet Piglet, the pot
felt much lighter, but for some reason, his
stomach felt heavier!

When Pooh arrived, Piglet had nearly finished digging the hole.

"Did you bring the honey?" Piglet asked.

"Yes," answered Pooh.

Pooh handed the honey pot to Piglet and together they placed it in the hole. The trap was all set.

It was getting late. Pooh and
Piglet decided to meet at their trap
in the morning. Then they would see
if they had caught a heffalump.

"Good night, Pooh," said Piglet.

"Good night, Piglet," said Pooh.

WHAT IS A HOUSE
WITHOUT HUNNY

Later that night, Pooh woke up with a rumbling in his tummy. It could only mean one thing—he was hungry!

So Pooh went to his cupboard for a pot of honey. But when he looked inside, his last pot was empty!

Where had all his honey gone?

"Oh, bother!" Pooh said.

Suddenly he remembered. He had left a pot of honey in the heffalump trap!

"Heffalumps like honey," said Pooh. "It will probably eat the whole pot!"

At least he thought it would.

WHAT IS A HOUSE WITHOUT HUNNY

Pooh could not fall asleep.
His empty tummy gave him strange
thoughts. He kept imagining heffalumps
chasing giant pots of honey!

The more he thought about it, the more
Pooh wondered if heffalumps really did
like honey, after all. And if they did not,
then the pot of honey in the trap would
still be there, just waiting to be eaten.
    So Pooh jumped out of bed and ran
out of the door.

Soon, Pooh reached the heffalump trap.

Pooh tried to see if there was a heffalump in the trap, but it was too dark to tell. So he moved closer to the hole.

But he still couldn't see, so he moved even closer.

And closer.

Until...

OOPS!
He fell into
the hole!

Pooh looked into the
honey pot and decided
that heffalumps did like
honey, because there was
only a little left in the
pot. Who else could have
eaten it?

Pooh stuck his nose
into the pot to lick the
last few drops.

At that very moment, Piglet was lying in
bed thinking about the heffalump.

"I wonder what a heffalump looks like?"
Piglet said to himself. "Is it very horrible?"

Piglet was quite worried. Heffalumps were very large and he was very small. What should he do?

"I don't have to be afraid," Piglet said at last. "He can't catch us while we're catching him!"

So first thing the next morning, Piglet ran
to the trap. Very slowly, he inched closer to
the hole. But he could not see anything.

So he moved a little closer.

Suddenly, Piglet saw a strange monster
with a big round head!

Piglet had never seen anything like
this before.

He was terribly excited!

"We've caught a heffalump!" he cried.
"Christopher Robin will be so happy!"

Piglet ran to Christopher Robin's house.
Piglet was so excited that he didn't even stop
to say hello. He just ran straight in.

"What is it, Piglet?" Christopher Robin
asked. He had never seen Piglet so excited.

"We've caught a heffalump!" Piglet shouted.

"You have?" asked Christopher Robin.

"Yes!" Piglet cried. "It has a big, strange
head the size of a honey pot!"

"Show me," urged Christopher Robin.

So Piglet took him to the trap.

Christopher Robin walked right up to the edge of the trap and looked in. Piglet stayed safely behind him.

"Oh, dear!" cried Piglet. "Can you see it? Can you?"

"Yes, I can, Piglet," answered Christopher Robin.

"Is it horrible?" Piglet asked excitedly.

Christopher Robin smiled and began to laugh. And he laughed and laughed.

Suddenly a loud noise came from the hole.
CRACK!
Piglet looked down and what did he see? Pooh!
Piglet had thought it was a heffalump, but it was
really Pooh with a honey pot stuck on his head!

Later that day, Christopher Robin, Pooh and Piglet had another picnic in the woods. It was a beautiful day, with the sun shining down on the three friends.

"We never did see a heffalump," said Piglet.

"That's okay," said Christopher Robin. "Heffalumps are rather shy, anyway."

"Yes," agreed Pooh. "Besides, I had no honey for it, and heffalumps love honey. At least I think they do!"

Christopher Robin laughed.

"Silly old bear," he said. "I love you both so much!"

Rabbits Howse

Piglet

Nise For Piknics

Sandpit where Roo playe

Owl

R SANDERS

Pooh Bears Howse →

Floody Place

100 Aker Wood